NOTE TO PARENTS

Learning to read is an important skill for all children. It is a big milestone that you can help your child reach. The Richard Scarry Easy Reader program is designed to support you and your child through this process. Developed by reading specialists, each book in the series includes carefully selected words and sentence structures to help children advance from beginner to intermediate to proficient readers.

Here are some tips to keep in mind as you read these books with your child:

First, preview the book together. Read the title. Then look at the cover. Ask your child, "What is happening on the cover? What do you think this book is about?"

Next, skim through the pages of the book and look at the illustrations. This will help your child use the illustrations to understand the story.

Then encourage your child to read. If he or she stumbles over words, try some of these strategies:

- **Use the pictures as clues**
- **Point out words that are repeated**
- **Sound out difficult words**
- **Break up bigger words into smaller chunks**
- **Use the context to lend meaning**

Finally, find out if your child understands what he or she is reading. After you have finished reading, ask, "What happened in this book?"

Above all, understand that each child learns to read at a different rate. Make sure to praise your young reader and provide encouragement along the way!

Introduce Your Child to Reading

Simple words and simple sentences encourage beginning readers to sound out words.

Your Child Starts to Read

Slightly more difficult words in simple sentences help new readers build confidence.

Your Child Reads with Help

More complex words and sentences and longer text lengths help young readers reach reading proficiency.

RICHARD SCARRY'S
Great Big Schoolhouse
Readers

Ice Cream
for Breakfast

Illustrated by Huck Scarry
Written by Erica Farber

STERLING CHILDREN'S BOOKS
New York

RING! RING!

"Hello," said Huckle

"Do you know what today is?"
asked Bridget.
"It's backward
day!"

Huckle walked backward up
the stairs.

He didn't see Sally. Oops!

Huckle put on his
shirt backward.

4

He put on his pants backward.

He put on his hat backward.
Lowly did, too.

Knock-knock! It was Bridget.
She was just in time for dinner.
Dinner is always before breakfast
on backward day.

First, they ate ice cream.

Then they ate pizza.

Yum! Yum!

They walked to the bus stop
backward.

They got on the bus backward.

But the bus driver made
them sit forward.
Thank you, bus driver!

Miss Honey asked them to write
their names backward.

E-L-K-C-U-H is Huckle spelled
backward.

Lowly thought hard about
how to write his name backward.
He broke the chalk!

At recess, Arthur went backward down the slide. "Oops!" he said.

"Spoo!" said Molly.

"That's *oops* spelled backward!"

Skip and Frances played
basketball backward.

Huckle and Lowly played
soccer backward.

Watch out! LAOG!

Then they all played
hide-and-seek backward.
"You found us. Now we'll go hide,"
said Bridget to Huckle.

"Three, two, one—ready
or not, here I come!" said Huckle.
"You mean one, two, three!"
said Bridget.

Then it was time for the class play.

It was the story of Cinderella.

The ending came first.

Here's how it went:

Cinderella married the prince.

Then she lost her slipper.

The clock struck midnight.

The fairy godmother turned the

pumpkin into a coach.

She turned two mice into footmen.

The evil stepmother handed
Cinderella a broom and told her
to clean.

The beginning was last.
Miss Honey clapped and clapped.

Everyone bowed backward!

Backward day was almost over.

Huckle had breakfast for dinner.

He had cereal and orange juice.

Then he put
on his pajamas
backward.

He brushed
his teeth
backward.

The toothpaste got on
his nose. CHOO-AH!

RING! RING!

"Hello," said Huckle.

"Do you know what tomorrow is?"
asked Bridget.

"Upside-down day! I'm doing a
headstand right now."

Huckle did a headstand, too.
He was so tired from going
backward all day.

He fell asleep upside down!

STERLING CHILDREN'S BOOKS
New York

An Imprint of Sterling Publishing
387 Park Avenue South
New York, NY 10016

In association with JB Publishing, Inc.

ISBN 978-1-4549-1312-2

Produced by

 JR Sansevere

Distributed in Canada by Sterling Publishing
c/o Canadian Manda Group, 165 Dufferin Street
Toronto, Ontario, Canada M6K 3H6
Distributed in the United Kingdom by GMC Distribution Services
Castle Place, 166 High Street, Lewes, East Sussex, England BN7 1XU
Distributed in Australia by Capricorn Link (Australia) Pty. Ltd.
P.O. Box 704, Windsor, NSW 2756, Australia

For information about custom editions, special sales, premium and corporate purchases,
please contact Sterling Special Sales at 800-805-5489 or specialsales@sterlingpublishing.com.

Printed in China

Lot #:
2 4 6 8 10 9 7 5 3 1
12/13

www.sterlingpublishing.com/kids

24

RICHARD SCARRY'S
Great Big Schoolhouse
Readers

One of the best-selling children's author/illustrators of all time, Richard Scarry has taught generations of children about the world around them—from the alphabet to counting, identifying colors, and even exploring a day at school.

Though Scarry's books are educational, they are beloved for their charming characters, wacky sense of humor, and frenetic energy. Scarry considered himself an entertainer first, and an educator second. He once said, "Everything has an educational value if you look for it. But it's the FUN I want to get across."

A prolific artist, Richard Scarry created more than 300 books, and they have sold over 200 million copies worldwide and have been translated into 30 languages. Richard Scarry died in 1994, but his incredible legacy continues with new books illustrated by his son, Huck Scarry.